W9-BDH-744

DANGER ON
MIDNIGHT RIVER

A YEARLING BOOK

Published by
Bantam Doubleday Dell Books for Young Readers
a division of
Bantam Doubleday Dell Publishing Group, Inc.
1540 Broadway
New York, New York 10036

ISBN: 0-440-41028-2

Series design: Barbara Berger

Interior illustration by Michael David Biegel

Printed in the United States of America

August 1995

OPM   20   19   18   17   16   15   14   13   12

Dear Readers:

Real adventure is many things—it's danger and daring and sometimes even a struggle for life or death. From competing in the Iditarod dogsled race across Alaska to sailing the Pacific Ocean, I've experienced some of this adventure myself. I try to capture this spirit in my stories, and each time I sit down to write, that challenge is a bit of an adventure in itself.

You're all a part of this adventure as well. Over the years I've had the privilege of talking with many of you in schools, and this book is the result of hearing firsthand what you want to read about most—power-packed action and excitement.

You asked for it—so hang on tight while we jump into another thrilling story in my World of Adventure.

Gary Paulsen

DANGER ON MIDNIGHT RIVER

CHAPTER 1

 Daniel Martin took one last look around his bedroom. It was pointless to put it off any longer. With a sigh he grabbed his suitcase, threw his sleeping bag up on his shoulder, and slowly walked outside.

The front screen door slammed behind him. He stood on the porch, ran his hand through his short brown hair, and looked up at the dark clouds in the sky. If he was lucky, there would be a storm and the whole dumb trip would be canceled.

He thought about his mom. He knew she

wouldn't be able to come and see him off. She was working. She was always working.

Daniel's mother was the day-shift waitress down at the Corner Cafe in town. It had taken her a year of scrimping and saving to get together enough money to send him to Camp Eagle Nest in the Premonition Mountains. This trip was so important to her. She said she wanted Daniel to have some fun for a change.

Daniel didn't want to go to any stupid camp. It wasn't that he didn't appreciate his mom's hard work, but he would rather have spent this summer the way he had every other summer since his dad had died five years earlier—in the Rocky Mountains with his uncle Smitty.

Uncle Smitty didn't treat him the way everyone else did. Up in the mountains it was understood that Daniel could take care of himself. He had spent a lot of time listening and learning about things that might mean the difference between life and death.

Daniel sighed again. That was another

world. In this world—this town world—he was his mama's baby boy. He was thirteen years old, but she insisted on driving him to school and kissing him goodbye every morning.

School wasn't much better. At school he was the class nobody. They called him things like nerd face and dork breath. It wasn't his fault he was a slow learner. For some reason, he just couldn't understand things as easily in school as when Uncle Smitty taught him stuff at the cabin. The teacher called him a student with special needs. Most of the kids called him retarded.

Daniel rounded the corner by the gas station in the center of town and looked up. His lanky frame stiffened. *Wouldn't you just know it? The Eagle Nest van is already here. The driver's probably one of those cheerful types who'll whistle and make jokes all the way to the camp.*

For a second he entertained the thought of going to the cafe and telling his mother that he'd missed the van. But knowing her, she'd work twice as hard so that she could get off early and drive him the seventy miles to the stupid camp.

No, he'd just have to tough it out. Uncle Smitty had told him it probably wouldn't be that bad. He'd said to try and have fun with it. *Fun—at a rich kids' camp for snobs. Sure, no problem.*

The driver was standing by the back of the van when Daniel walked up. "You're late, squirt. Give me your gear and let's get this show on the road."

Daniel shrugged and handed him his suitcase. *So much for the cheerful type.*

The large man practically ripped the sleeping bag out of Daniel's hand. "I said let's go, kid. I don't get paid by the hour. This is my first trip as a driver for the camp and I don't want no foul-ups." He shoved the boy toward the sliding side door of the van.

"Well, well. Look who's here. Daniel the dork."

Daniel paused on the second step and looked up into the pudgy face of Scotty

Howard. His worst nightmare had just come true. Scotty and his friends Troy Dennis and Brandon March were the only other passengers in the van.

Troy was big for his age, with an attitude to match. He looked out the window. "Where's your mama, Danny boy? Ain't she gonna come down and kiss you bye-bye?" Troy and Scotty howled with laughter.

Brandon let his feet slide off the seat in front of him. They hit the floor with a thud. His dark blue eyes narrowed and he scowled. "Leave him alone, boneheads. Let him get in the van."

"Aw come on, Brandon." Scotty held his hands out. "We're just trying to have a little fun with the geek."

"Later." Brandon's face was serious.

"Whatever you say, O wise one." Scotty moved out of the aisle to let Daniel pass. As Daniel took a step, Scotty stuck his foot out and tripped him. Daniel fell to his knees.

He jumped up with his fists clenched. "Try that again, lard bucket."

"Not in my van." The driver growled as he pulled the sliding door shut. "You peacocks can fight all you want after you get there. For now find a seat and sit in it. Don't even think about getting out of it before we get to the camp." Climbing in behind the wheel, the driver turned toward them. "I also don't want no music, loud talking, or snoring." He mumbled something under his breath about spoiled rich kids and started the engine.

Daniel moved to the last seat at the back of the van. He propped himself in the corner and pretended to go to sleep.

Scotty sat down in the seat in front of Daniel and whispered, "I wouldn't sleep too soundly, Danny boy. You never know when the boogey man might get ya."

Troy and Brandon spun around in their seats two rows ahead. Troy laughed. "Watch it, Scotty, you're scaring him. We may have to stop and get his teddy bear out of his suitcase."

Brandon rubbed his eyes and took a pack of

cards out of his back pocket. "Why don't you idiots grow up?"

Scotty leaned back over the seat. Daniel could feel the boy's hot breath on his face. "You're gonna love camp, Danny boy. I'm gonna see to it personally."

CHAPTER 2

 The storm was steadily growing worse. Giant drops of rain pounded the van with a vengeance. The driving wind buffeted the van and made it hard to stay on the road.

Daniel stared anxiously out the window. They had been driving in the mountains for several hours. He looked at his watch. They should have been there by now.

He glanced at the three boys laughing and playing cards in the middle of the van. They were acting as if they didn't have a worry in the world.

The driver was a different story. Beads of sweat dripped off his forehead. His knuckles were white from clutching the steering wheel so hard. Daniel could tell that the man could barely see the road, and more often than not the van veered over onto the shoulder.

Abruptly the van left the pavement and began traveling on a dirt road. Daniel looked at his watch again. They hadn't passed a car in more than an hour. He considered asking the driver if they were lost, then decided against it. If they were, there wasn't anything Daniel could do about it anyway.

From the hollow sound the van made as it passed over the wooden planks, Daniel could tell they were on some sort of bridge.

The driver scratched his head and muttered under his breath. "Don't remember no bridge out here. Musta made a wrong—"

Suddenly it felt as if they were flying. The plank noise was gone and the van soared effortlessly through the air.

When it hit the water, it hit hard. The boys were thrown against the walls like rag dolls.

The van was instantly sucked into the raging current and dragged downstream.

The driver was hanging limply over the steering wheel. Blood trickled from the corner of his mouth. Outside, the rain still hammered down. The heavy front end of the van was completely submerged, and only the back stuck out of the water as the churning river drove it down the treacherous canyon.

Daniel opened his eyes and shook his head. It felt as if he'd been kicked by a mule. His forehead throbbed and he could feel a knot on it. He raised himself up and tried to see outside. The back end of the van was slowly sinking.

There was only one chance. Crawling to the back door, he unlocked it and pushed it open. The rain pelted him and the wind forced him back. He braced himself and shoved.

It was an immediate fight for his life. The angry water hurled him down the river as if his body were no more than a stick.

Daniel was a strong swimmer, but the swift-moving current was too much for him. It was all he could do to keep his head above the surging water. A couple of times he thought he heard someone yelling. But for now he had his own problems. The river was freezing cold, and it offered no way out.

CHAPTER 3

Branches clawed at his face and clothes. He reached up and locked his right arm around one. The current yanked his legs underneath the tree. Daniel held on. With what little strength he could muster, he inched his way up the tree trunk to the bank.

The rain had turned to drizzle. Daniel lay on the bank exhausted. It was getting late, and he was chilled to the bone. He didn't know how long he'd lain there before he finally opened his eyes. More than anything he would have liked to stay there and rest, but a nagging voice inside his head was telling him he had to keep moving. It was cold and there was a risk of hypothermia.

Daniel pulled himself into a sitting position and surveyed his surroundings. In front of him was the river. It was dangerously high, with no apparent way back across. Behind him and up the short canyon bank was forest as far as the eye could see.

The rain had soaked almost everything in sight. Building a fire to dry out would be quite a trick, even using everything Uncle Smitty had taught him. Daniel moved up the mountain a few yards away from the river. Sitting under an evergreen, he dug through the wet, dead leaves until he found some dry needles and a couple of dead branches.

He carried them up the hill and sat down under a large tree that had branches thick enough to protect his precious tinder from the drizzle. Reaching into his pocket, he drew out a pocketknife and cut away the outer bark of the dead branches until he had completely dry wood. With his hands he dug until he had a fire pit. He arranged the dead leaves and needles in a teepee shape.

Daniel took a deep breath. *So far so good.*

Going back to the bank, he walked up and down until he found a good-sized piece of chert, a shiny black rock. He scooped it up and ran back to his campsite.

Holding the rock near the dead needles and wood shavings, he struck it with the back of his knife blade. Sparks flew, but nothing caught.

Seven times he tried before a tiny spark ignited the end of a dead needle. Daniel blew gently until there was a small blaze. Then he added more wood shavings and finally a branch.

He left the fire to search for more wood. When he had enough to keep the fire going for a while, he took off his shoes and socks and put them close to the flames to dry.

He leaned back against the mountainside with his toes toasting near the fire. Its warmth felt good. He was almost asleep when he heard it.

Yelling.

He sat up on one elbow. Before, he had been so worried about himself that he had completely forgotten about the rest of the van's passengers.

The thought of going out in the rain again made Daniel shudder. But he knew it was the right thing to do. He built up his fire, then slipped on his damp socks and shoes and stepped out from under the protection of his tree.

The yelling was coming from downriver. The van must have passed him while he was lying on the bank. He ducked his head and trotted to keep from getting chilled again.

About fifty yards downriver he found them. The current had slowed and lodged the van on some boulders near the middle of the river. Only a small piece of the van's white top showed above the water.

Scotty was lying half out of the water, coughing and vomiting on the rocky bank. Brandon was frantically swimming around the van, trying to get a door open.

When Scotty saw Daniel, he pointed at the van. "Troy! He's still in there!"

Daniel didn't hesitate. He kicked off his shoes and jumped into the water. When he got to the van, Brandon screamed, "Troy's hurt but he's still alive! The door's stuck and I can't get him out!"

Daniel dove under the water. He tried to pull the back door open, but it was wedged tight against a rock. He quickly swam to the side door and rammed his shoulder into it. It moved, but not enough.

Daniel held on to the mirror and kicked the door. It popped open. He went to the surface for a quick gulp of fresh air and then dove back down.

Inside the van he saw the driver still hanging lifelessly over the steering wheel. Daniel searched for Troy and found him floating at the top of the water near the back of the van.

Daniel's lungs felt as if they were about to burst. He grabbed Troy under the arms and worked his way out the door. Holding on to

Troy with one hand, he fought his way to the surface.

"He's not breathing," Daniel said between gasps. "He'll need mouth-to-mouth. Help me get him to shore."

CHAPTER 4

Daniel built the fire up until he had a roaring blaze. He had put Troy as close to the fire as he dared, hoping it might help to bring him around.

Troy was breathing, but he was still unconscious. His skin was light blue, and he was shivering. Daniel rubbed Troy's hands and arms. He turned to Brandon. "Dig down under that tree over there and bring me all the dry leaves, moss, or grass you can find. And hurry."

Brandon didn't question him. In a few minutes he returned with an armful of dry leaves and grass. Daniel began stuffing them inside Troy's clothing and packing them around him. "It'll help insulate him from the cold."

Daniel continued to rub Troy's feet and legs. When Troy's socks were dry Daniel put them back on him. He felt Troy's forehead. It was hot.

Scotty looked a little better and was now resting against the huge tree watching Troy anxiously. "Is he gonna die?"

Daniel didn't look up.

"Is there anything I can do?" Brandon asked.

"You can get us a supply of wood. The main thing is to keep him as warm and dry as possible."

"I can help." Scotty started to stand.

"You take it easy." Brandon pushed him back down. "I'll get it."

Scotty watched Daniel work. "How do you know all this stuff? I mean I've seen you in class. You're no Einstein."

Daniel shrugged. "Most of what I'm doing is

just common sense. Besides, Brandon's the one who did the mouth-to-mouth."

Troy moaned softly. His eyes opened. "Where . . ."

Scotty moved to him. "It's okay. There was an accident. The van fell in the river. Danny boy here pulled you out."

Troy looked over at Daniel. His mouth turned up in a feeble grin. "Thanks."

"I was in the neighborhood."

Brandon came back with an armload of wood. "Hey. Nice to see you in the land of the living again. I thought there for a minute you were gonna check out on us."

Troy coughed. "Me too."

Daniel shook out his handkerchief and headed for the river.

"Wait up." Brandon jogged up to him. "Where you going?"

"Troy's still not out of danger. He needs hot liquids." Daniel dipped his handkerchief in the water until it was dripping wet and quickly ran back to the fire. He held it over the flames until it was warm.

Daniel told Troy to open his mouth, and he let the warm water drip in until he had squeezed the handkerchief dry. Then Daniel stood up to repeat the process.

Brandon took the handkerchief. "I'll do it this time."

The two boys took turns until Daniel was satisfied that they had done all they could. He felt Troy's forehead again. It wasn't quite as hot.

Daylight gave way to darkness, and the only light came from the fire. The rain started up again, but the boys were fairly well protected under the branches of the big tree.

Scotty and Troy were sleeping soundly. Daniel added a good-sized stump to the fire so that it would burn all night, then cleared a place to stretch out.

Brandon threw a handful of pine needles into the fire. "You're okay, you know."

An awkward silence filled the night. Daniel stared into the flames. "Most people are—if you give them half a chance."

CHAPTER 5

Brandon sleepily yawned and opened his eyes. It was midafternoon and the sun beat down on him. He sat up and stretched.

A small fire was still burning. A large rock with a hollowed-out center sat near the edge of it. Something liquid was boiling in it. To the side of the fire was a generous pile of pinecones.

Scotty and Troy were still asleep. Daniel was nowhere in sight. Brandon shook Scotty's ankle. Scotty turned over and opened one eye. "What?"

"Wake up. It's the middle of the day."

Scotty rubbed his eyes and sniffed the air. "I'm starved. What's cooking?"

Brandon shrugged. "I don't know. Daniel must have left it. Looks like water with chopped-up pine needles in it."

"It's tea." Daniel stepped out from behind a tree. The front of his T-shirt was filled with round green berries.

He dumped the berries on a grassy spot. "It's made from pine needles. Has more vitamin C than orange juice." Using his handkerchief, he tipped the rock and let some of the liquid run into a piece of bark he had carved out with his knife. He held it out to Scotty. "Try some."

Scotty took the bark. "I'm game." He sipped the hot liquid. "Not bad."

Brandon picked up one of the pinecones and tossed it into the air. "What are we gonna do with these? Have a war later?"

"Those are part of your breakfast." Daniel held one of the cones over the fire. When it was warm he easily popped off some of the scales. "See these little winged-looking seeds?" He put them in his mouth. "They're good."

"These don't taste all that great." Daniel pointed to his little cache of berries. "But they'll help fill the empty place in your stomach."

Scotty stripped off a few of the berries and tossed them in his mouth. "Danny boy, you are amazing."

A small rock flew through the air and hit Scotty in the chest. Troy sat up and smiled. "You dummies gonna keep all the grub to yourselves or what?"

Scotty threw the rock back. "I think I liked you better when you were unconscious."

Daniel poured some of the tea for Troy. Troy reached for it, and some of the leaves and pine needles fell out of his shirt. He looked at Daniel. "Would it be okay with you if I un-stuffed myself? I feel like a scarecrow. This junk is kinda uncomfortable."

Daniel nodded. "I don't think you need it anymore. But you still ought to take it easy today."

"Does that mean you think we should wait another day before we try finding our way out of here?" Brandon asked.

Daniel nodded again. "Troy wouldn't get too far before we'd have to stop and make another camp, and besides"—he looked up at the sky—"it's a little late in the day to start."

Scotty popped some scales off his pinecone. "Why don't we just stay where we are? Someone's bound to find us sooner or later. Until they do, Troy can rest up."

"They don't know where we are." Daniel poured more tea for Troy. "The way I figure it, the driver took a wrong turn about an hour out of town. After that he just kept going. We should have been at Camp Eagle Nest two hours after we left yesterday, but we were still driving after about four hours."

"You mean we're not even close to the camp?" Scotty's voice rose slightly.

Daniel shook his head. "We could be anywhere. I think the driver knew we were lost and he kept trying different roads hoping to get back on course."

"What are we going to do?" Troy asked.

"We have three choices. One is to sit here, build a signal fire, and wait. We can hope someone sees it and comes to get us. The second is to walk up this side of the river to the place where the bridge washed out and see if the road leads anywhere."

"What's the third thing?" Brandon asked.

"The third thing is the most dangerous, but if it works it'll get us home the fastest. We go downstream and find the slowest-moving part of the river and try to get to the other side. Follow the river back upstream to the bridge and then follow the road home."

"Not me." Troy shook his head. "Ain't no way this boy is getting back in that water. Forget it."

Brandon looked at Daniel. "Which way do you want to take?"

"Back across the river."

CHAPTER 6

Several hours later Daniel dropped his wood by the fire. It was strangely quiet around the camp. Scotty nudged Brandon with his elbow.

Brandon cleared his throat. "We, ah, we took a vote while you were gone."

Daniel was silent.

"It's just that we think it makes more sense to stay on this side of the river. I mean, it's safer and that road on this side of the bridge has to lead somewhere, doesn't it?"

"We don't want to go against you or anything, Danny boy." Scotty looked sheepish.

"We appreciate everything you've done and all, but Troy's a little nervous about the water, and to tell you the truth, so am I."

Daniel knelt by the fire. He didn't look at them. His voice was low. "What if it doesn't lead to anything? It could just be an old forest road the rangers use to check on things up here."

"We think it's worth a try," Brandon said.

Daniel stood and wiped his hands on his jeans. "Maybe it's for the best. If we split up, one of us is bound to find help sooner or later."

"We don't necessarily have to split up," Brandon said. "Unless you want to."

"Like I said, it's probably for the best."

Troy touched Daniel's shoulder. "No hard feelings?"

Daniel shook his head. He looked up at the night sky. *Well, at least I was the hero for a little while. I should have known these guys didn't really want me around. To them I'm still Daniel the nerd.*

Scotty punched him in the arm. "As soon as

we reach civilization we'll come looking for you, Danny boy. Promise."

Daniel put a log on the fire. He stretched out on the ground and turned over so that they couldn't see his face.

"Right," he said quietly.

CHAPTER 7

Daniel sat on his heels and watched the water. He had walked downriver for more than two and a half miles, until he'd found a likely-looking spot at which to cross. He had been watching it for a long time. It didn't look too deep, and the current appeared to be slow enough that he could get across without too much trouble.

He thought about the three boys back at the camp and how, for a little while, things had been different among them. For the first time he could remember, Daniel had actually felt like part of a group. Then they had turned on him.

They had all been asleep when he had silently withdrawn this morning. He had purposely left early so that he wouldn't have to face their empty goodbyes.

Daniel looked at the sky. Dark clouds were forming to the east. It would probably rain before afternoon. He smiled. With any luck, he would be halfway home before it hit.

Still, he didn't move to cross the river. He knew he was stalling. His thoughts kept going back to the trio on the mountain. He doubted they even knew how to start a fire.

Why should I care? Daniel suddenly stood up and stepped out into the water.

He stopped and thought of what his uncle Smitty would say about his leaving three helpless boys stranded on the mountain.

On the other hand, there's really no rush. Maybe I'll just hang around up here for a while.

"You and your big ideas." Brandon paused and looked around them. "Some shortcut,

Scotty. We've been walking for hours, probably in circles. Why do I ever listen to you? We should have crossed the river like Daniel said."

"Nobody stopped you." Scotty was breathing hard. "You weren't too anxious to swim across that river last night."

"That's because last night I was dumb and listened to you two. Daniel knows what he's doing. Didn't you see him? He fed us and kept us dry. Not to mention the fact that he saved Troy's life."

Troy sat on a log. "Let's take a break. I'm beat. We can argue all we want but it doesn't help our situation. We're lost." A drop of rain the size of a quarter hit him on the nose. "Great. This is all we need."

"Come on." Scotty led the way through the brush. "We need to get under a tree like the one Daniel found, before we get soaked."

As if on cue, the heavens opened and unleashed a furious downpour. Before they could take ten steps it was raining so hard it was difficult to see where they were going.

The boys crashed through the brush and dove under the first big tree they came to.

The only problem was, the space under the tree happened to be occupied. The little striped animal stamped its feet and hissed in warning. Then it whirled and in a flash sprayed them with foul-smelling liquid.

Scotty got the worst of it right in the face. He screamed and ran back into the rain, holding his hands over his eyes in pain.

Brandon grabbed Scotty's arm and pulled him to another tree Troy had found a few yards away. They huddled together near the base of the tree while the wind blew sheets of rain at them. They were helpless. There was nothing to do but cover their heads and wait the storm out.

Chapter 8

Daniel sat back and took a sip of his rainwater tea. The rain was beginning to let up. When it was clear enough he would try to pick up the boys' tracks again. Strangely, Brandon, Troy, and Scotty had left the river and cut across the mountain. Their tracks had led him over the tops of two ridges. There was no telling how far they had gone before the rain had hit.

He felt edgy. The newspaper was full of stories about backpackers who had lost their way up here. The Premonition Mountains were famous for catching inexperienced hikers unaware.

Daniel had never hiked up here. He didn't know these mountains at all. But thanks to the time he had spent with his uncle, he knew there was little chance of his losing his way.

He wished he could say the same for Brandon and the others. *What are they doing?* In the direction they were going they would never cut across the bridge road.

The air was cool, but he was anxious to get started. Taking handfuls of dirt, he doused the little fire. He knew it would be next to impossible to find any tracks after the rain. The best he could hope for was that the boys would continue in the same direction and break off branches here and there, leaving a trail that he could follow.

It was slow going. He circled and circled, hoping to find some sign of where they had gone. The noise he was making startled an old doe. She jumped out in front of him and bounded away.

Daniel smiled. *Some backwoodsman. I'm louder than a herd of buffalo.*

The doe drew his attention to some brush off to his right. The bushes had been trampled recently and hadn't had a chance to recover. Daniel pushed some of them aside. Under one was the clear imprint of a tennis shoe, now filled with muddy water.

He looked in the direction the boys appeared to be heading. It didn't make sense. Why would they try to cross the Premonitions —unless they were lost? If they were, it would make his job even harder. They could change direction at any time.

Daniel wondered if he had made a mistake. Maybe it would have been better for him to cross the river and get help instead of wandering around up here. He cupped his hands and yelled for the others.

There was no answer.

He decided to keep going. If he lost their trail now, he might never be able to find them.

When the van didn't show up at Camp Eagle Nest, he figured, they'd send out search parties. A lot would depend on how wide an area they covered. The searchers wouldn't be able to spot the van at all now. On his trip downriver he had discovered that it had completely sunk below the surface.

Anyway, he doubted if a search party would think to look on this side of the mountain range. The more he thought about it, the more he was convinced that the driver had taken them close to a hundred miles in the wrong direction.

Daniel worked the area carefully. He cut their trail again near an ancient pine tree. The dirt and pine needles under the tree had been packed down. He studied the place where the three boys had waited out the rain, and scratched his head.

The tree was on the wrong side of a small ravine. They had been sitting facing the wind as it drove the heavy rain in at them. To stay dry, all they would have had to do was move to a tree on the other side of the ravine, or move around to the other side of this tree.

These guys are worse off than I thought. They don't even have enough sense to come in out of the rain.

From the tree, the tracking became easier. The boys had walked in the mud and left a good clean trail. Daniel followed it up a rocky slope. From there they had taken a ninety-degree turn and moved parallel with a rock cliff.

Daniel paused at the top of the cliff and looked out. Below him was a sheer drop. In front of him were miles and miles of forest. It was a forbidding sight.

The possible urgency of the boys' situation jarred him back to reality. It was getting late and he still hadn't been able to catch up with them. Which meant they would probably spend a cold, sleepless night without food or water.

Part of him felt as if they deserved it. But another part remembered the way Brandon had defended him in the van, and the look on Troy's face when he'd tried to thank Daniel for saving his life.

He kept going.

CHAPTER 9

Brandon was awake. He had dozed fitfully but had been awake most of the night. His T-shirt was still damp from yesterday's rain. And he still had no idea where they were. Slapping his arms to warm himself, Brandon looked at the sky. "Come on sun."

Scotty squinted up at him. "You couldn't sleep either?"

Brandon shook his head. "Too cold. How're your eyes?"

"They still sting. But that's not what's keeping me awake. I'm starving. I've been trying to get these stupid pinecones to open up, but they won't."

"Daniel said you have to hold them over the fire. And since we don't have one . . ." Brandon looked around. "Where's Troy?"

Scotty rubbed his eyes. "He said he had to go to the john."

"How long has he been gone?"

"Come to think of it, he's been gone a pretty long time."

Brandon cupped his hands. "Troy!"

There was no answer.

"Come on." Brandon helped Scotty to his feet.

Scotty stumbled after him. "You don't think he's lost, do you?"

Brandon just looked at him.

"Right," Scotty said.

Brandon moved along the cliff yelling Troy's name. "Wait." Brandon stopped. "I think I hear something."

A muffled voice came from below the cliff edge. "Help me! I'm down here!"

Brandon ran to the edge and looked over. "Troy, what happened?"

Troy was sitting on a rock ledge a few feet below. His leg didn't look right. It was thrust out to his side at an odd angle.

"I stepped wrong and the whole world fell in. I think I busted my leg. Lucky for me this ledge was here or I'd be a goner."

"Can you move it?"

Troy shook his head.

Brandon searched for a way down. Though the distance was only a few feet, there wasn't one. "Scotty, you hold my feet. I'm going to hang down there and try to pull him up."

"Are you crazy? I can't hold both of you."

"You got any better ideas?"

"I do." Daniel stepped out onto the cliff.

The boys turned. Relief washed over Brandon. "If there was ever anybody I was glad to see, it's you."

Scotty squinted at him. "Is that you, Danny boy? I thought you'd be halfway home by now."

"And miss all the fun?" Daniel looked over the edge of the cliff. "How's the weather down there?"

Troy gave him a halfhearted grin. "Don't tell

me. You just happened to be in the neighborhood, right?"

"Something like that." Daniel turned. "You guys hand me your belts."

Daniel pulled his belt off, tied it to the other two, and jerked the slack out of them. He handed one end to Brandon. "Lie down and hang on to this. Scotty, you hook your foot around that bush and hold Brandon's feet."

Holding one end of the belt rope, Daniel scooted to the edge of the cliff and lowered himself to the ledge below.

One look at the angle of Troy's leg told him it was broken. Daniel shook his head. "Some people will do anything for attention."

"I'd be real happy to share this kind of attention, believe me."

Daniel moved around to stand behind Troy. "There's only one way to get you out of here. I'm going to help you stand on your good leg. Then grab the belt and Brandon and Scotty will pull you up. Ready?"

Troy nodded.

Daniel bent down, lifted Troy under the

arms, and helped him hop to the belt rope. "No matter how much it hurts, you have to hang on, okay?"

"You're the boss." Troy took the end of the belt rope in both hands.

Daniel motioned with his thumb. "He's ready. Pull him up."

Inch by inch Brandon pulled. The jagged rocks tore at Troy's flesh and ripped his clothes, but he hung on. When they got him to the edge, Brandon grabbed his arm and dragged him up and over the lip of the cliff.

"Okay, now me," Daniel called. He was easier to pull up because he could help with his legs. When he reached the top he went over to Troy and felt his lower leg. "You really did a job on this. Hang on, I'll be right back."

Troy's face was white from the pain. "I'll be here."

Daniel moved off the rocky slab and found two sticks about the same length. He tore a strip off the bottom of his T-shirt and trotted back to where Troy was lying.

"This is going to hurt some."

Troy gritted his teeth. "Do what you have to do."

Daniel straightened the leg as gently as he could. Troy winced and drew a sharp breath. Daniel put a stick on either side of the leg and wrapped them in place with the strip from his shirt.

"That's the best I can do for now."

He tied the last knot, then moved upwind and sat on the rock slab. "I hate to mention this, but you guys really stink."

Scotty stepped around Brandon. "We had a little run-in with a skunk last night."

"Smells like the skunk won."

Brandon rubbed the back of his neck. "We kinda made a mess of things. I don't suppose . . ."

Troy raised himself up on one elbow. "What he's trying to say is, since you left we haven't had anything to eat and we don't have a clue where we are."

"How about it?" Scotty asked. "Want to get three hardheads out of the woods?"

Daniel stood up and brushed off the back of his jeans. "If we're going to get out of here, it's going to take all of us." He looked at Troy. "Especially since Troy has decided he'd rather ride than walk."

CHAPTER 10

 Daniel directed the building of a makeshift stretcher. They found two long branches and pulled the smaller limbs off. Using their belts, their shoelaces, and strips off their T-shirts, they tied shorter branches across the two longer ones.

Daniel filled in the cracks with pine boughs. He made a mock bow in front of Troy. "Your carriage awaits." Scotty and Brandon lifted Troy from the ground and carefully placed him on the stretcher.

Daniel intended to stick to his original plan and cross the river at its slowest-moving point. He checked the sun and started back in the right direction. The boys took turns carrying the stretcher throughout the day. Daniel gathered edible grasses and berries, and they ate as they walked.

When it was nearly dark, Daniel motioned for them to set the stretcher down under a tree. Troy's face was still white. His eyes were closed and he was obviously in pain.

"Sorry I can't offer you anything to drink." Daniel cleared a place for a campfire. "But tomorrow we'll be at the river and you can drink your fill."

Scotty lay back in the dirt. "I'm done. I don't think I can walk another step."

"How long will it take us to get home after we get to the river?" Brandon asked.

Daniel blew on twigs and pine needles to start the fire. "It depends on how long it takes us to get across and how far it is back upriver to the washed-out bridge."

"I heard something." Scotty sat up. "It's coming from over there." He pointed out into the gathering darkness. "There it is again. Something's in that brush."

Brandon sat up. "Bears?"

Daniel moved behind the fire and picked up a sturdy round stick.

A large brown dog trotted out into the opening. He stopped when he saw the fire and the boys.

"Oh, it's just a mutt." Scotty held out his hand. "Here, boy."

"Don't call him." Daniel eyed the dog. "Everyone stay perfectly still. Don't give him any reason to come this way."

The dog lowered his head and growled. He took a step toward them and hesitated.

Brandon cautiously reached for a stick. The dog snarled and bared his teeth. White foam dripped from his mouth.

Troy felt around on the ground beside him. His hand rested on a large rock.

The dog pawed the ground like an angry bull. He shook his head and some of the white slobber flew off. For a minute it looked as if he was going to turn and go back into the bushes.

Suddenly he charged straight for them, lunging at Daniel. Daniel quickly sidestepped and brought the stick around. He nailed the dog on the back of the head, knocking him to his knees.

Troy raised his rock and brought it down squarely on the dog's head. The dog didn't move. Daniel stepped closer, his stick still raised.

The dog wasn't breathing.

Daniel poked it with his stick. "You got him, Troy."

"I don't understand." Scotty looked bewildered. "Why did he act like that?"

Daniel moved back to the fire. "Rabies."

Brandon pointed his stick at the dog. "He could have killed us."

Daniel nodded. "If he had bitten one of us, we probably wouldn't have lasted more than a couple of days."

Scotty was still staring at the dog. "I wonder what he's doing way out here?"

"No telling." Daniel put a piece of wood on the fire. "He probably made it to this side before the bridge washed out, picked up the disease, and couldn't figure out how to get back."

Scotty nervously looked out into the darkness. "What if he bit something else?"

"He probably did. That skunk you guys told me about, for instance. Skunks don't usually roam around in the daytime unless something's wrong."

A shudder went through Scotty. "This place gives me the creeps. The sooner we get home the better."

CHAPTER 11

 When they reached the river, Daniel made them boil the water before he let them drink, to eliminate any possibility of contamination from diseased animals. Then they drank until they thought they would burst.

After a short rest, they carried Troy downstream until Daniel found the place where he had wanted to cross.

Again Daniel sat and watched the water, searching for any telltale signs of drop-offs or other hidden dangers.

"What are you waiting for?" Brandon came up behind him. "It looks okay to me."

"You're probably right, but it never hurts to check." Daniel threw a rock into the water. "You and I will make sure Troy gets across and we'll let Scotty worry about the stretcher, okay?"

"Sounds like a plan to me."

Daniel stood up. "Let's get started."

Brandon and Daniel lifted Troy off the stretcher while Scotty slipped it out from under him. Scotty wrapped his arm around the first rung of the stretcher and stepped out into the water.

Daniel looked at Troy. "All you have to do is float. Brandon and I will do the rest."

Scotty shouted at them from the middle of the river. "I'm still standing. It's not that deep here."

"Hear that, Troy?" Brandon patted his shoulder. "Piece of cake."

They stepped down into the water. Daniel moved to the lead and put his arm under Troy's chin to keep Troy's head up. Brandon stepped to the side to help push Troy through the water.

"Sure beats swimming." Brandon looked down at Troy. "We're almost there."

Daniel turned to look back at them. As he did, he stepped into a bottomless hole. He lost his hold on Troy and sank below the water. Brandon reached for Daniel to pull him back up.

The current grabbed Troy. The upper part of his body was floating away. Troy's leg was useless, so he tried to use his arms to swim. He splashed frantically, trying to get turned around. Brandon snatched at him and managed to hang on to Troy's shoe for a second, but it quickly slipped out of his hand.

Daniel broke the surface of the water and gasped for air. He swam wildly in Troy's direction and grabbed the front of his shirt. "Gotcha."

Troy hung on to him. His voice trembled. "I thought you guys said this would be a piece of cake."

Brandon helped turn him around.

"We lied."

CHAPTER 12

"I see it. There it is."

The boys had made it to the bank and were following the river back to the bridge. Brandon pointed excitedly. "We found it," he announced to the others.

Daniel and Scotty followed him up a rise. They laid Troy down and walked to the bridge. Now that it wasn't raining, it was easy to see that part of the bridge was missing. There was a gaping hole in the center. The three boys looked over the edge and stared at the swift-running water below.

"It's amazing any of us are still alive."

Scotty looked downstream. "It's too bad about the driver. I wonder if they'll ever find his body."

"They'll find him." Daniel stepped back. "When we get back we'll give them the approximate location of the van. It probably hasn't moved that much. It was stuck pretty good."

Daniel reached for his end of the stretcher. "We better keep moving, it's getting late. With any luck we could run into a car sometime tomorrow."

Scotty sighed and picked up his end. "The first thing I'm going to do when I get back is take a long, hot soak in the tub."

Troy raised his head. "I'm going to the hospital—and after that I'm going to have the biggest cheeseburger in town."

"I'm going to fall into my water bed and sleep for a thousand years." Brandon looked at Daniel. "How about you? What's the first thing you're going to do when you get back?"

Daniel looked embarrassed. "First I'm going to make sure my mom knows I'm all right." He glanced up at Scotty. "She kinda worries about me. Then I guess I'll go home and call my uncle Smitty and tell him all about our time up here."

Scotty shifted the weight of the stretcher. "There's something I've been meaning to tell you, Danny boy." Scotty hesitated. "All that stuff I said earlier. You know that stuff on the bus about your mom—well, I was being a jerk."

"Me too." Troy smiled. "But Scotty was the biggest jerk."

"You won't get any argument from me." Brandon thumped both of them on the back of the head.

Two tiny lights flickered in the distance. They moved closer.

"I see it, but I don't believe it." Daniel moved to the center of the road. "It's a truck."

The headlights grew larger until a light-green truck stopped in front of them. A forest ranger stepped out. "By the looks of things, I'd say you boys must be the lost campers."

Brandon clapped Daniel on the back. "Are you kidding? Daniel here knew where we were all the time."

The ranger helped them put Troy in the bed of the truck. "Looks like you had a rough time, son."

Troy shook his head. "Naw. Not with Daniel around. He's the one who set my leg."

The ranger looked at Daniel. "Sounds like these guys were lucky you were along."

Scotty stepped up. "We probably wouldn't have made it without him."

The ranger smiled. "There's a reporter from one of the big papers waiting back in town. I'm sure he'll be very interested in how you boys survived the Midnight River."

"Reporter?" Scotty slid into the front seat with the ranger. "Did I say we wouldn't have made it without Daniel? What I meant to say was that I was a big part of getting us out alive. Yes sir. A very big part." Scotty was still talking as he slammed the door.

Brandon looked at Daniel and shrugged. "So he's still a jerk, what can I say?" He jumped up into the back of the truck. "With friends like us, you'll have to stay on your toes."

Daniel stepped up into the truck bed. He

looked through the window at Scotty, who was still talking the ranger's ear off. Troy and Brandon were discussing what a pain Scotty was.

Daniel wasn't really listening. He had stopped at the word *friends*. . . .

GARY PAULSEN

ADVENTURE GUIDE

RIVER SURVIVAL

Always study the movements of any stream or river you are about to cross. The current in the middle of a river is faster than the current closer to the banks. But even next to shore, chances are the current is not flowing evenly. Try to locate eddies (areas of backward-flowing water), rapids, or bottomless holes, which could trap you.

If you become caught in swift-moving water, turn on your back with your feet pointing downstream to deflect rocks or other obstacles. Keep your legs up; do not attempt to stand. Watch for branches or logs that you can grab on to to keep you afloat. If the water calms, turn on your side and swim for shore.

Get out of cold water as fast as you can, and take every measure possible to get warm. The threat of hypothermia is real. Hypothermia is a condition in which the body temperature drops below normal and heat is lost faster than the body can produce it. Symptoms of hypothermia include slurred speech, blue or white skin, and uncontrollable shivering. To combat hypothermia, raise the body's temperature by sitting near a fire, drinking hot liquids, wrapping the body in warm clothing, or stuffing dry leaves between the skin and damp clothing.

If you must cross unfamiliar water, do not cross at a certain place simply because it is where your path meets the river. Take time to seek out the safest place to cross.

Look for these thrill-packed adventures coming soon!

The Gorgon Slayer

Eleven-year-old Warren Trumbull has a crazy job. He works for Prince Charming's Damsel in Distress Rescue Agency, saving people from hideous monsters, evil warlocks, and wicked witches. One day Warren gets the most dangerous assignment of all: He must exterminate a Gorgon. Warren will need all his courage and skill—and a surprise weapon—to become a true Gorgon slayer.

Captive!

When masked gunmen storm into his classroom, Roman Sanchez and three other boys are taken hostage. They are hauled to a run-down mountain cabin, bound with rope, and given no food. With each passing hour the kidnappers' deadly threats become more real. Roman knows time is running out. He and the other boys must pull together now and launch a last desperate fight for freedom.